CONTENTS

WHAT IS A PLANT?

Plants are living organisms that are usually fixed in one place. They produce energy by harnessing the power of sunlight.

A WORLD OF PLANTS

There are more than **390,000 different species** of plants in the world.

PLANT CELLS

Like all living things, plants are made from **cells**. Like animal cells, plant cells have a **nucleus**, which contains the **genetic** instructions, and **mitochondria** that turn **sugars** into **energy**.

The nucleus contains the genetic instructions for the cell in a long strand-like chemical called deoxyribonucleic acid (DNA).

Jelly-like cytoplasm fills the inside of the cell.

The vacuole is a space inside a plant cell that contains sap.

Ribosomes are tiny structures in which proteins are made.

Mitochondria produce energy using sugars and oxygen in a process called respiration.

Unlike animal cells, plant cells have a rigid cell wall made from tough cellulose.

Chloroplasts contain a chemical called chlorophyll, which harnesses sunlight to produce sugars.

The cell membrane is the outer layer of the cell and controls what goes in and out.

PHENOMENAL
PLANTS

First published in Great Britain
in 2019 by Wayland
Copyright © Hodder and Stoughton, 2019
All rights reserved

Editor: Amy Pimperton
Text written by Rob Colson and
Jon Richards
Produced by Tall Tree Ltd
Designers: Malcolm Parchment and
Ben Ruocco

HB ISBN: 978 1 5263 0782 8
PB ISBN: 978 1 5263 0783 5

Wayland
An imprint of Hachette Children's Group
Part of Hodder and Stoughton
Carmelite House
50 Victoria Embankment
London EC4Y 0DZ

An Hachette UK Company
www.hachette.co.uk
www.hachettechildrens.co.uk

Printed in China

PHOTOSYNTHESIS

Plants play a vital role in life on Earth. They use the energy of sunlight to convert **carbon dioxide** and **water** into **sugars** and **oxygen**.

The chemical reaction that takes place in **photosynthesis** looks like this:

$$6CO_2 + 6H_2O + sunlight = glucose\ (C_6H_{12}O_6) + 6O_2$$

C stands for carbon
O stands for oxygen
H stands for hydrogen

MAKING OXYGEN

The oxygen plants produce through photosynthesis is vital to all living things on the planet.

A single human breathes about **740 kg** of oxygen every year – this is roughly the amount of oxygen produced by **7 trees**.

Water

Sun

Sunlight

Glucose

Carbon dioxide

Oxygen

.... *Fern*

Vascular plants have special tubes inside them to transport water and nutrients. Vascular plants can grow very big. They include **ferns**, **clubmosses**, **flowering plants** and **conifers**.

.... *Moss*

Non-vascular plants do not have an internal system of tubes to transport water and nutrients. Because of this, they do not grow big. Examples include **liverworts** and **mosses**.

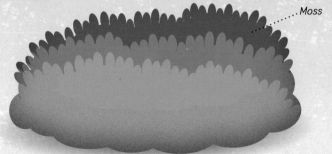

PLANET HABITATS

Climate conditions, location on the planet and the type of rock and soil determine what types of plant can grow in a region and the habitats that are found there.

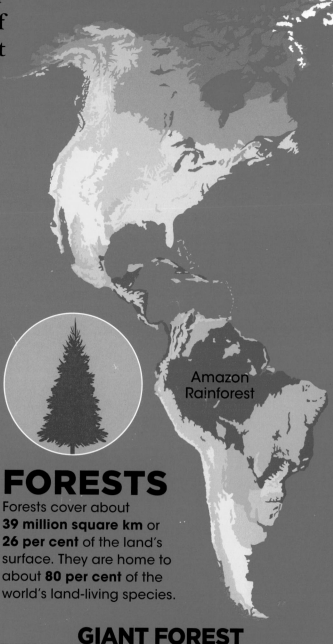

LAND ZONES

Land covers about **29 per cent** of Earth's surface. The **World Wildlife Fund** divides this into eight major **habitats**, or **biomes**. Forests are subdivided into three habitats and grasslands into two different habitats.

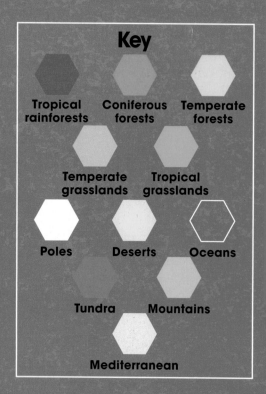

Key

Tropical rainforests

Coniferous forests

Temperate forests

Temperate grasslands

Tropical grasslands

Poles

Deserts

Oceans

Tundra

Mountains

Mediterranean

Amazon Rainforest

FORESTS

Forests cover about **39 million square km** or **26 per cent** of the land's surface. They are home to about **80 per cent** of the world's land-living species.

GIANT FOREST

The **Amazon Rainforest** contains half of Earth's total rainforest. It covers an area of 5.5 million km².

GRASSLANDS

These cover about **40 per cent** of the planet's land area (excluding **Antarctica**). **Grasses** are the dominant plants.

NORTHERN GRASS

The **Eurasian Steppe** is an enormous area of grassland that stretches about 5,000 km from Hungary in Europe to East Asia.

Greenland

Eurasian Steppe

Sahara

HOT AND DRY

The **Sahara** covers an area of 9.2 million km².

DESERTS

These are the driest places on Earth, with less than **250 mm** of rain every year. Any plants that live here are adapted to cope with long periods without water, such as the thick, succulent stems found on **cactuses** to store water.

Antarctica

TREES

Trees are the giants of the plant world. They are found on every continent on the planet, except for chilly Antarctica.

TOP TO BOTTOM

- The **crown** is the top part of a tree, made up of the spread of the **limbs** that grow out from the **trunk** including the branches and leaves.
- The **trunk** is the main stalk or stem of the tree.
- The **roots** are the underground parts of a tree. They draw up water and nutrients from the ground and hold the tree in place.

TALLEST TREES

	Height (m)
A **coast redwood** named Hyperion (California, USA)	115.92
A **mountain ash** named Centurion (Tasmania, Australia) (see page 27)	99.82
A coast **Douglas fir** named Doerner Fir (Oregon, USA)	99.7
A **Sitka spruce** (California, USA)	96.7

Crown

Branch

Limb

Trunk

Trunk is covered in bark.

Leaves grow on narrow twigs.

Roots can extend deep underground.

The tree with the deepest roots is a wild fig that grows in dry areas in South Africa.

ITS ROOTS

grow deep to find water, and have been found in caves 120 metres underground.

Hyperion
115.92 m

Centurion
99.82 m

Doerner
99.7 m

Redwood

Mountain ash

Fir

SUCKING UP WATER

Inside the trunks of trees are tiny tubes. Using a process known as **capillary action**, water is drawn up the tubes to all parts of the tree, sometimes more than 100 metres above the ground.

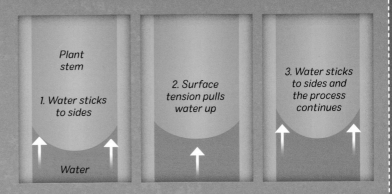

Plant stem

1. Water sticks to sides

Water

2. Surface tension pulls water up

3. Water sticks to sides and the process continues

FAST GROWTH

The foxglove tree is one of the fastest growing trees in the world. It can grow more than **30 cm** in **3 weeks** (an oak tree will grow this much in a whole year). It also produces **3–4** times more **oxygen** than any other tree.

LARGEST CROWNS

Width (m)

A **coolabah** tree named Monkira Monster (Queensland, Australia)....... 72.8
An **oriental plane** tree (Wiltshire, UK) 64.0
A **raintree** named Samán de Güere (Aragua State, Venezuela) 63.1
A **silk-cotton** tree named Big Tree (Barro Colorado Island, Panama) 61.3

In comparison a football pitch is about 60–70 m wide.

Sitka 99.7 m

96 m

Spruce

Elizabeth Tower, London (the clock tower that houses Big Ben)

GRASSES

Huge areas of land are covered by some of the youngest plants on the planet – grasses. These incredible plants are also very useful, supplying a large amount of the food we eat.

GRASSLAND

There are two main types of grassland: **tropical** and **temperate**. Tropical grasslands, such as the African savanna, have a dry season and a wet season, and are warm all year. In the wet season, about 250 cm of rain falls. Temperate grasslands, such as the Eurasian Steppe, have up to 75 cm of rain a year, with warm summers and cold winters.

Temperate grassland

Tropical grassland

ANIMALS

Grass grows from the **base**, rather than the **tip**. This means that grasses can be trampled over and the tops cut off by grazing animals without killing the plants. As a result, grasslands can produce enough food to support **enormous herds** of animals.

North America

Prairies

Europe

Africa

Savanna

South America

Pampas

Node

Leaf

Crown

NEEDED

Some **35 species** of grass have been domesticated, including the four main cereal crops – **wheat**, **barley**, **rye** and **oats**. More than 50 per cent of the world's food comes from grasses.

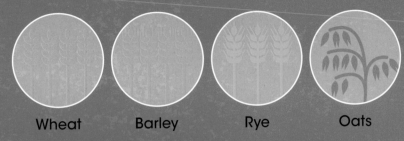

Wheat   Barley   Rye   Oats

LATE ARRIVAL

Grasses are some of the **newest** plants on Earth. The first land plants appeared more than **400 million** years ago, but grasses only appeared about **60 million** years ago.

GIANT GRASS

Bamboo is a huge kind of grass that is the **fastest-growing** plant on the planet. Some species can grow at up to **4 cm** an hour.

<︙·············· 4 cm ··············>

actual size

Asia

Eurasian Steppe

India

Bamboo is both strong and flexible

Savanna

Australia

Rangelands

Antarctica

TOUGH GRASS

Bamboo is incredibly tough and is used as **scaffolding** in some parts of the world.

TALL GRASS

The tallest grass in the world is the giant bamboo, which grows in India. It can reach up to **46 metres** high.

46 m

KILLER PLANTS

These plants are dangerous to be around. Some like to feed on animals, while others produce some of the deadliest toxins on the planet to stop animals from eating them.

DEADLIEST PLANTS

These are six of the deadliest plants and their **symptoms** (if eaten):

- **Water hemlock** causes painful convulsions, abdominal cramps, nausea and death.
- **Deadly nightshade** causes paralysis of body muscles, including the heart, and death.
- **White snakeroot** causes nausea, abdominal pain, reddened tongue, abnormal blood acidity and death.
- **Castor bean** causes vomiting, diarrhoea, seizures and death.
- **Rosary pea** causes organ failure and death.
- **Oleander** causes vomiting, diarrhea, seizures, erratic pulse, coma and death.

WARNING: Never eat plants in the wild. They may be poisonous.

Deadly nightshade grows in Europe and North Africa. It is related to the tomato, but its leaves and berries are highly poisonous. In ancient Europe, the poison was used to make deadly weapons.

MEAT-EATERS

Some plants that live in **poor soil** supplement their diet by eating meat!

The traps of a **bladderwort** can swing shut in as little as **20 milliseconds!** Blinking your eyes can take 150 milliseconds.

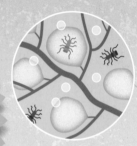

Bladderworts are aquatic plants that suck prey into their traps.

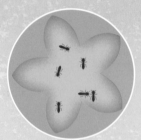

Butterworts have sticky leaves that insects cannot escape.

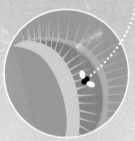

Venus flytraps have jaws that snap shut on unsuspecting visitors.

The largest **carnivorous** plant is
NEPENTHES RAJAH,
a type of pitcher plant whose pits can grow more than **40 cm high** and **20 cm wide** and are big enough to trap and consume rats! It will also eat frogs, lizards and even birds!

Pitcher plants have pitfall traps that creatures fall into.

FIENDISH FIGS
Strangler figs use other larger plants, such as trees, for support. They grow around the host tree and often kill it, leaving behind a hollow structure made from their own stems.

A strangler fig grows around another tree's trunk

DEADLY DARTS
In South America, people make deadly darts using the **toxin, curare**. Made from tree bark, curare kills its victims by **paralysing** their muscles, which stops them from breathing.

13

STINGING NETTLES
Nettles are covered in tiny stinging hairs. When you brush up against them, the hairs inject toxins into your skin.

Stinging hairs

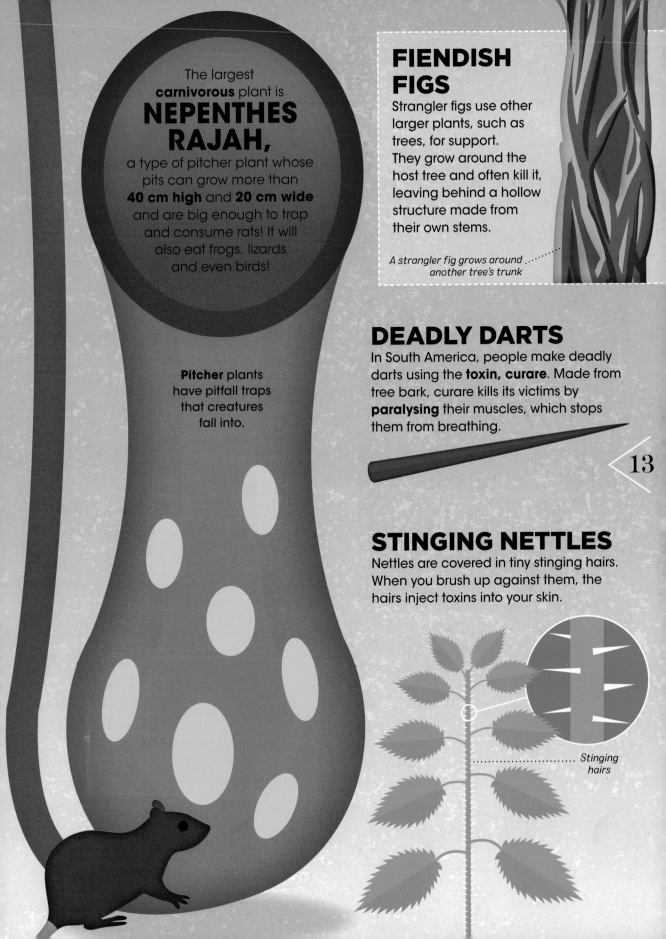

IN BLOOM

Flowers come in a huge range of sizes and colours and use their incredible displays to attract animals to pollinate and fertilise them.

WHAT IS A FLOWER?

A flower is the part of some plants involved in reproduction. They contain both the male and female parts, and these come together during fertilisation to make seeds.

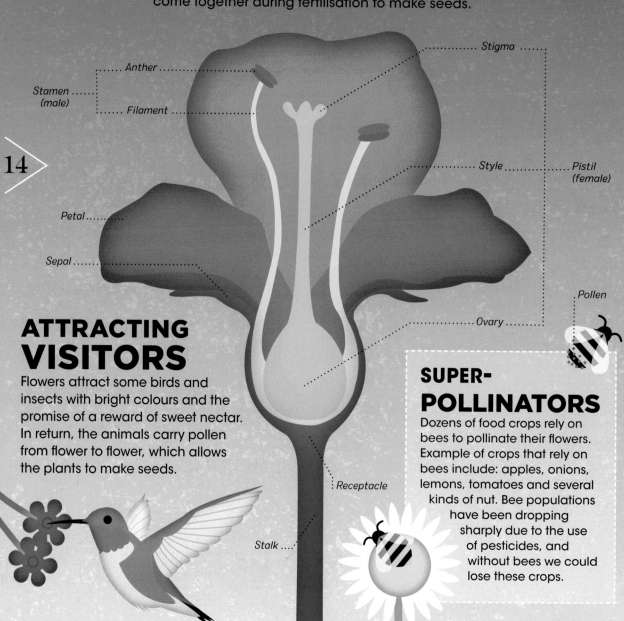

Stigma

Anther

Stamen (male)

Filament

Style

Pistil (female)

Petal

Sepal

Pollen

Ovary

Receptacle

Stalk

ATTRACTING VISITORS

Flowers attract some birds and insects with bright colours and the promise of a reward of sweet nectar. In return, the animals carry pollen from flower to flower, which allows the plants to make seeds.

SUPER-POLLINATORS

Dozens of food crops rely on bees to pollinate their flowers. Example of crops that rely on bees include: apples, onions, lemons, tomatoes and several kinds of nut. Bee populations have been dropping sharply due to the use of pesticides, and without bees we could lose these crops.

Wisteria flowers

WISTERIA

A wisteria planted in 1894 in California, USA, has grown to cover about **4,000 square** metres (about 2.5 times the area of an ice hockey rink). Every year it produces more than 1.5 million flowers weighing more than **200 tonnes**.

SMALLEST **FLOWER**

The smallest flower in the world is produced by the water-meal plant, or *Wolffia globosa*. These tiny aquatic plants are less than a millimetre long. 5,000 of them could fit in a thimble.

The vanilla cactus in Mexico blooms for just **ONE NIGHT** each year. Its white flowers open up one evening then wither the very next morning.

BIGGEST **FLOWERS**

Rafflesia arnoldii measures **1 metre** across and weighs up to **11 kg**. It produces a smell like rotting flesh to attract flies. It is also known as the '**stinking corpse lily**'. The titan arum flower can reach **4 metres** tall.

Rafflesia arnoldii produces flowers that measure about 1 metre across and weigh about 7 kg.

The titan arum *produces a spike-like flower that can be 4 metres tall and weigh 75 kg.*

FIRST FLOWERS

One of the oldest flowering plants in the world is *Amborella trichopoda*, a rare shrub found in New Caledonia in the South Pacific. Scientists believe that it evolved about 130 million years ago. This is around the time flowering plants first appeared on Earth.

LEAVES

Leaves are found on the stems of vascular plants. These flat or pointy plant parts come in many shapes, sizes and colours, but they all play a vital role in keeping plants alive.

TYPES OF LEAVES

Broadleaf or **deciduous** trees have flat leaves that turn brown and drop off in winter. **Evergreen** trees have thin, needle-like leaves that stay on the tree all year round.

MAKING SUGARS

Leaves are the main places where **photosynthesis** takes place. The energy of sunlight is used to convert carbon dioxide and water into oxygen and sugars.

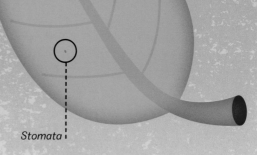

Stomata open

LOSING WATER

Leaves help to regulate the loss of water from the plant through tiny holes, called stomata, on the underside of the leaves.

Stomata

········*Guard cell*

Stomata closed

Guard cells around the stomata can open and close to control the flow of gases and water into and out of the plant.

SHINY LEAVES

In tropical rainforests, plants have to cope with a lot of water. Their leaves often have a smooth, shiny surface to allow water to run off them.

The tropical plant Monstera deliciosa has shiny leaves with holes in them to help water to drain away. It is also known as the Swiss Cheese plant.

A TONNE OF LEAVES

Each spring, a large oak tree will grow about **200,000** leaves.
Together, the leaves weigh about **1 tonne** – the weight of a family car.

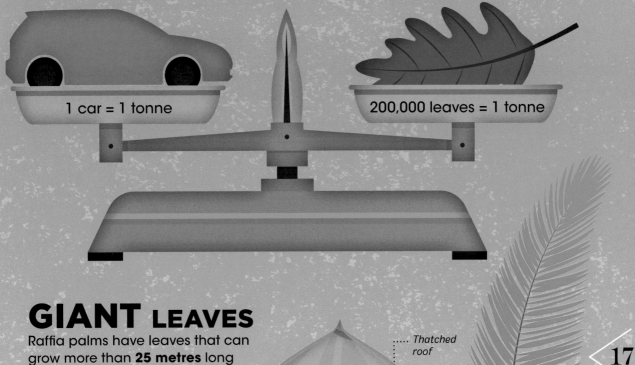

1 car = 1 tonne

200,000 leaves = 1 tonne

GIANT LEAVES

Raffia palms have leaves that can
grow more than **25 metres** long
and **3 metres** wide. The dried
membranes on the underside
of the leaves are made into
raffia fibre, which is used to
make rope and textiles and
to thatch roofs.

..... Thatched
roof

..... Raffia
palm

TINY LEAVES

The leaves of the common water fern
measure less than **1 mm** long. Each leaf
traps a pocket of air, and this helps to
keep the plant floating at the surface,
where it forms a dense
green carpet.

.... Water ferns

FRUIT AND VEGETABLES

Many plants produce edible parts that are used to attract animals to eat them. The animals spread the plant's seeds around by discarding the inedible parts or passing these parts through their poo.

FRUIT OR VEG?

The simplest way to tell the difference between a fruit and a vegetable is that a fruit has **seeds**.

Vegetables include other edible parts of plants, including their **roots**, **leaves** and **stems**.

However, we think of many fruits, such as **tomatoes**, **courgettes** or **cucumbers,** as vegetables.

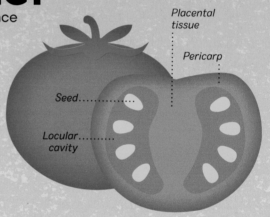

Placental tissue

Pericarp

Seed..............

Locular cavity..........

Stamen cluster

Fleshy mesocarp

Pericarp

Seed

POMEGRANATES

Pomegranates contain more seeds than any other fruit – up to **1,400.**

PRICEY FRUIT

The world's most expensive fruit is the **Yubari King** cantaloupe melon. Only produced in the Yubari region in Japan, it is valued for its extreme sweetness. Two were sold for **3 million yen (£20,000)** in Japan in 2016.

SPUDS IN SPACE

Potatoes were the first vegetables grown in space, when **NASA** and the **University of Wisconsin-Madison** joined forces on a mission in October 1995.

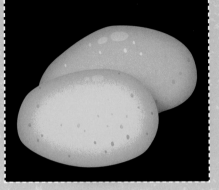

PONGY FRUIT

The **Durian**, which grows in southeast Asia, is said to be the world's **smelliest** fruit. It has an odour of **rotten eggs**, **sweaty socks** and **rotting rubbish**. Despite its stench, some people think it is delicious, but others are disgusted by it. It is banned from public places in Singapore.

EXTREME FRUIT AND VEG
These are some truly gigantic examples:

The pumpkin is a member of the squash family.

A giant pumpkin weighed in at **1,190.5 kg,** which is almost the weight of two adult cows.

Cabbage heads can be green, purple or white.

A cabbage weighed in at **62.71 kg,** which is about twice the weight of a Dalmation dog **27–32 kg**

Garlic is closely related to onions.

A lemon weighed in at **5.265 kg,** which is about the weight of a cat

A large courgette is often called a marrow.

A courgette weighed in at **29.25 kg,** which is about the weight of **5** bowling balls.

A garlic head weighed in at **1.19 kg,** which is slightly less than the weight of the human brain.

SEEDS AND BULBS

Some plants produce bulbs and seeds to reproduce. Some plants also go to extremes to make sure their seeds will grow.

NEW SEEDS

Seeds are produced by the merging of male and female **cells** from different plants. This process is called **fertilisation**. The fertilised seed contains an **embryo**, which is the young plant, and a food store to help the embryo to grow in its first few days.

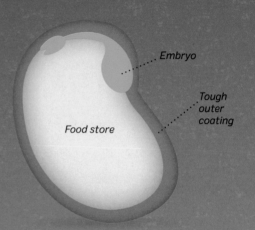

Embryo

Tough outer coating

Food store

FOOD STORE

Bulbs grow **underground** and provide a store of food for a plant. They can also grow into new plants that have just one parent and are **genetically identical** to the parent plant.

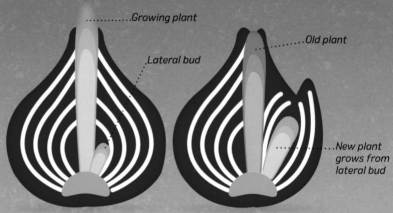

Growing plant

Old plant

Lateral bud

New plant grows from lateral bud

BIGGEST SEED

The largest seeds in the world are made by **coco de mer** palm trees. The seeds can measure **50 cm** across and weigh up to **25 kg**.

The coco de mer seed can float across oceans.

BIGGEST BULB

The **candelabra lily**, or **Josephine's lily**, grows from bulbs that are **25 cm** wide. The bulbs sit on top of the soil and grow from there.

ANCIENT SEEDS

In 2012, scientists grew new plants from seeds of *Silene stenophylla* – a Siberian flower – that were **32,000** years old. The seeds had been buried by a squirrel near the banks of the Kolyma River in Russia.

LONG-DISTANCE VOYAGE

Plants distribute their seeds in many different ways, using the wind, sticking to animals, or through an animal's poo. Some plants even distribute their seeds across oceans. Seeds from the tropical vine, Mary's bean, grow in a few places in **Central America**. One seed drifted on ocean currents to the shores of **Norway**, a distance of **24,000 km**.

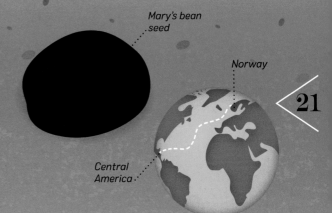

Mary's bean seed

Norway

Central America

TULIP MANIA

Across the winter of 1636–1637, the Netherlands was gripped by a craze for tulips. Prices for tulip bulbs soared, and a single bulb of a rare tulip could sell for more than **4,000 Dutch guilders** – more than **10 years'** wages for an average worker!

However, when spring arrived, demand for the bulbs fell and the prices for them quickly crashed, making many people very poor.

Average tulip bulb prices in guilders: (November 1636–May 1637)

250
225
200
175
150
125
100
75
50
25
0

1 November 1636

1 May 1637

OLDEST PLANTS

Plants have been around on Earth for a very long time. The earliest plants were single-cell algae that floated in the oceans more than a billion years ago. Individual plants can be very long-lived, and some have been alive since prehistoric times.

PANDO

Pando, a **colony** of **identical male** quaking aspen trees that all share the same root system, in Utah, USA, is thought to be 80,000 years old. Each individual tree lives for about **130** years.

All the trees are male and genetically identical to one another.

Seagrass is a flowering plant that lives underwater.

SEAGRASS

A colony of seagrass in the Mediterranean Sea is estimated to be anywhere between **12,000–200,000** years old.

LIVING FOSSIL

Ginkgo trees in China are the oldest known **living fossils** (living things that were alive during prehistoric times and are still around today). Fossils of ginkos exist from the **Jurassic Period (140–200** million years ago), meaning that they lived alongside giant dinosaurs, such as *Apatosaurus*.

On old trees, needles only grow at the ends of a few branches.

Ginkgo tree

Bristlecone pines grow very slowly in dry, stony soil.

Apatosaurus

OLD TREE

The world's oldest individual tree is a bristlecone pine in the White Mountains, California, USA. It is **5,067 years old** and its location is kept secret to protect it.

THE EVOLUTION OF **PLANTS**

First evidence of photosynthesis – about **3 billion** years ago.

First land plants – about **450 million** years ago.

Early seed ferns – about **375 million** years ago.

First flowering plants – about **200 million** years ago.

First grasses – about **60 million** years ago.

SMALLEST PLANTS

These plants may be some of the smallest on Earth, but they can cover huge areas of the planet and play an important part in our climate.

WOLFFIA

Wolffia, also known as **duckweed** or **water meal**, is the smallest flowering plant on the planet. The entire plant is about **0.6 mm** long and **0.3 mm** wide. A dozen of them would fit through the eye of a needle.

Wolffia also produces the world's smallest fruit, but the fruit is also the biggest in relation to its parent plant, taking up a third or more of the parent's length.

Sewing needle

Wolffia

Salt

Wolffia seed

Salt grain

MINIATURE TREE

The dwarf willow is considered by many scientists to be the smallest tree in the world. It grows up to a maximum of **6 cm** tall and its leaves are only about **1 cm** wide. The tree's tiny size helps it to survive in harsh conditions in the Arctic and on high mountains.

Dwarf willow leaf

<·1 cm·>

Actual size

SMALL BUT IMPORTANT

Tiny ocean plants play a vital role in Earth's carbon cycle. They take **carbon dioxide** from the air as part of photosynthesis. Each year, ocean plants transfer about **10 billion tonnes** of carbon from the atmosphere into the ocean. This helps to **limit global warming** by reducing the amount of the **greenhouse gas**, carbon dioxide, in the atmosphere.

Phytoplankton
can form
**GIANT
BLOOMS**
that are visible
from space.

MICROSCOPIC PLANTS

Plankton are **tiny organisms** found in fresh water and salt water. Some of them, called phytoplankton, are single-celled plants, or algae. When conditions are right, the numbers of these organisms can explode, creating huge blooms that cover **hundreds** of **square kilometres**. They play an important part in the ocean food web as other living things, such as fish, feed on them.

Giant blooms of phytoplankton can be harmful to other sea life, as some produce **harmful toxins**. Also, when the blooms die, they sink to the bottom and decompose, reducing the **oxygen content** in areas of the water to the extent that other things can't live in it, creating '**dead zones**'.

Ocean covered with algae blooms

Land mass

BIGGEST PLANTS

These huge monsters have grown to super-size in order to stand taller, wider and generally bigger than the other plants around them.

BIGGEST

The largest living tree in the world is a giant sequoia called **General Sherman**. It grows in the **Sequioa National Park** in the USA and is **83.8** metres tall, weighs about **1,814** tonnes and has a volume of **1,487** cubic metres – enough to make **5 billion** matches!

Each match = **1,000,000,000**

Árbol del Tule

WIDEST

The thickest tree ever recorded is a **Montezuma Cypress** from Mexico known as **Árbol del Tule**, which measures **57.9 metres** in circumference. It would take about **40 people** holding hands to encircle the entire tree.

TALL PLANTS

Vascular plants can grow much taller than non-vascular plants. The tallest plants of all are trees, but even ferns and grasses can reach giant proportions.

Ferns on Norfolk Island in the Pacific Ocean can reach 20 metres tall – the height of a **six-storey** house.

Some species of bamboo can reach 30 metres tall – the height of a **nine-storey** building.

General Sherman
83.8 m

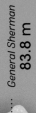

GIANT MOSS

On a slightly smaller scale, the largest moss is *Dawsonia superba* from New Zealand. This non-vascular plant can grow up to **60 cm** tall.

The tallest flowering plant is *Eucalyptus regnans* (mountain ash) in Australia, one of which has reached a height of 99.82 metres – that's equivalent to a **30-storey** skyscraper (see page 8).

EXTREME FARMING

Plants play a vital role in feeding the world, either directly as food for people, or as food for farm animals. Since farming started, the number of people on the planet has increased dramatically and farming methods have changed to produce food. We have developed crops, such as wheat and rice, which don't appear in the wild.

EARLY FARMING

About **10,000** years ago, the first agriculture developed in an area in the Middle East called the **Fertile Crescent**. Farmers grew and harvested wild grain.

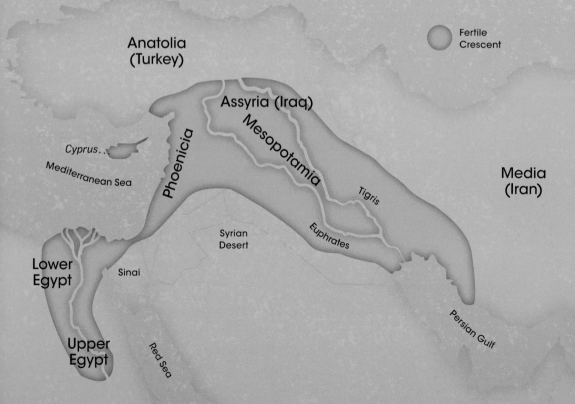

Anatolia
(Turkey)

Fertile
Crescent

Assyria (Iraq)

Mesopotamia

Cyprus

Phoenicia

Mediterranean Sea

Media
(Iran)

Tigris

Syrian
Desert

Euphrates

Lower
Egypt

Sinai

Persian Gulf

Upper
Egypt

Red Sea

WHEAT

About **8,000** years ago, **common wheat**, which is used to make bread, first appeared in southwest Asia from a hybrid (mixture) of **emmer wheat** and **goatgrass**.

RICE

About **6,500** years ago, two species of rice (**Asian rice** and **African rice**) had been developed.

MOST PRODUCED CROPS AROUND THE WORLD

Sugarcane	1.8 billion tonnes
Maize/corn	885 million tonnes
Rice	723 million tonnes
Wheat	701 million tonnes
Potatoes	373 million tonnes

THE BIGGEST RICE PRODUCERS ARE

China	195.714 million tonnes
India	148.26 million tonnes
Indonesia	64.399 million tonnes
Bangladesh	47.7 million tonnes
Vietnam	38.725 million tonnes

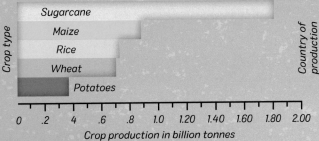

Crop type

Sugarcane
Maize
Rice
Wheat
Potatoes

0   .2   4   .6   .8   1.0   1.20   1.40   1.60   1.80   2.00

Crop production in billion tonnes

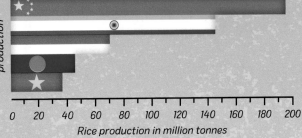

Country of production

0   20   40   60   80   100   120   140   160   180   200

Rice production in million tonnes

Each farm in the USA **FEEDS** on average 165 people.

MEGA MACHINE

New Holland's CR10.90 is the largest combine harvester in the world. Its tank can hold **14,500** litres of grain, equivalent to **200** bathtubs.

MEGA FARM

The world's biggest farm is the **Mudanjiang City Mega Farm** in Heilongjiang, China. It is a dairy farm with more than **100,000** cows, and covers an area of **9,000** square km – about the same area as **Cyprus**.

.... Cyprus

1 x COW = **10,0000**

GLOSSARY

ALGAE
Tiny plants that grow in water and lack stems, roots or leaves.

BARK
The tough outer covering of a tree. It protects the inner parts of the trunk and branches, reducing water loss and preventing damage caused by animals.

BULB
Found on some plants, this is a short base part of the stem that acts as a food store during non-growing months.

CAPILLARY ACTION
The process by which surface tensions causes water to rise up very thin tubes. Plants use capillary action to draw water up from the ground.

CELL
The smallest part of a living thing that can function on its own. Plants and animals are made up of millions and millions of cells.

CELLULOSE
A substance that forms the main ingredient of plant cell walls, making them stiff.

CROWN
The topmost part of a tree, which is made up of the branches, twigs and leaves.

DESERT
The name given to a region that receives less than 250 mm of precipitation (rain, snow or hail) in a year. Deserts can be hot, such as the Sahara, or cold, such as Antarctica.

EMBRYO
The name given to the developing young of living things. For example, plant embryos are found inside seeds.

EVOLUTION
The process by which living things change their appearance and behaviour. These changes can take a very long time over several generations and are usually in response to a change in the surrounding environment.

FERTILISATION
The joining of male and female sex cells to produce the cell that will grow into a new living thing.

GENETIC
Something relating to the genetic information stored in the cells of living things. This genetic information is stored in the form of deoxyribonucleic acid (DNA) inside each cell's nucleus.

HABITAT
This is the natural environment in which a living thing lives.

MITOCHONDRIA
Tiny rod-shaped structures found inside the cells of living things. They are the main sites where sugars and oxygen are combined to produce energy.

NON-VASCULAR PLANTS
Plants that do not have a network of tubes (called the xylem and phloem) to transport food and water around them. They include mosses and algae.

NUCLEUS
The central part of a cell inside which the DNA is stored.

PHOTOSYNTHESIS
The process by which plants use sunlight, carbon dioxide and water to produce sugars. At the same time, the process releases oxygen into the air.

PHYTOPLANKTON
The name given to water-living organisms that photosynthesise. They include algae.

POLLINATOR
An animal that carries pollen from one plant to another.

RAINFOREST
A forested region that receives a lot of rain all year round.

RESPIRATION
A chemical process by which living things produce energy from sugars and oxygen.

SPECIES
A group of living things that look and behave in the same way and produce fertile young that can have young of their own.

STEPPE
A large area of grassland that stretches from eastern Europe and right across Asia.

STOMATA
Holes on the underside of leaves that control the passing of gases and water into and out of a plant.

TAIGA
The name given to a large band of coniferous forest that stretches across northern parts of Asia, Europe and North America.

TEMPERATE
The name given to parts of the world that lie nearer the poles than the tropical regions.

THIMBLE
A small cap that fits over a fingertip. It is used when sewing to protect the finger when using a sharp needle.

TROPICAL
The name given to parts of the world that lie near the Equator.

VASCULAR PLANTS
Plants that have a network of tubes (called the xylem and phloem) to transport food and water around them.

INDEX